The Oogas at the Park

Written by
Denise M. Fleming, M.Ed.

Illustrated by
Lisa M. Sutton, MBA

Colored by
Laurel Berkel

The Oogas at the Park

Published by Clovercroft Publishing, Franklin, Tennessee

Illustrated by Lisa M. Sutton

Colorization and Interior Layout Design by Laurel Berkel

Printed in the United States of America

ISBN: 978-1-948484-15-2

This book is dedicated to Sharon Sterk. We came up with this character for a 4th grade Reading assignment. We created the character and then wrote up a story for our assignment. We took it a few steps further and told people we were Oogas that came down from Mars—that's the original planet we used. There was even an Ooga language we used to try and convince people we were really Oogas disguised as humans. We had a lot of fun with it. The character came back to me in early adulthood when I became a mother. I shared the story with my children and later my students. I decided to use this adorable character to write a book series about a very important rule that all should follow. It has been the number one rule in my home as well as my classroom.

I also want to dedicate this book to my sister, Lisa, who made this character come alive. Her illustrations were perfect! They went way above my expectations. The success of this book will be largely contributed to her artistic and creative ability.

Hi! I'm Shooga! I live on the planet, Benevolent. Do you know what "benevolent" means? It means to be kind to others. Here on our planet, we strive to live by the Blue Rule. I think it's called the Golden Rule on your planet. It says that we should treat others how we want to be treated.

My friends and I like to go to school to learn, and we play Oogarami at the playing field. And when we aren't in the classroom or on the field, we like to have fun playing at the park, just like you!

One day, my friend and I were going to the park to play.
We both love to swing and talk for hours.
My friend's name is Rooga. Oh, and I'm Shooga!

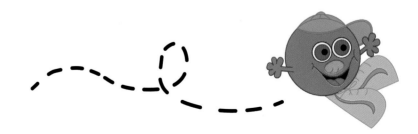

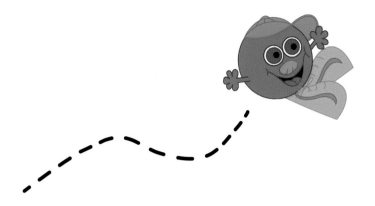

Rooga and I live close to the park, so we usually walk there. When we got there I asked him, "What do you want to do first, Rooga?"

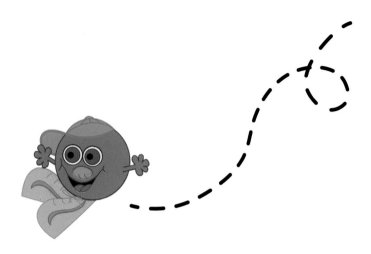

Rooga said, "Let's go down the slide ten times; then climb up to the top of the jungle gym; go down the slide five more times; go across the monkey bars; then we can eat our snack!"

So, we climbed up the slide and slid down it ten times. Then we climbed to the top of the jungle gym, and just as we were about to go down the slide five more times, our other friend Tooga came by.

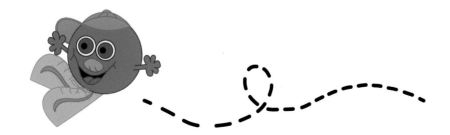

He ran up to Rooga and said, "Rooga! My mom is going to take me to the movies and said I can bring one friend! Do you want to come?"

"Sure!" Rooga replied.

Then he turned to me and said, "See ya later, Shooga!"

So, I gathered up the snack and headed home, alone.

When I walked through the door, my mom could tell something was wrong. She asked, "Why are you home so early from the park?"

"Rooga decided to go to the movies with Tooga," I replied.

"Did you get to eat your snack?" asked my mom.

"No," I said.

"Are you upset about something?" asked my mom.

"I am!" I exclaimed. "We were having so much fun at the park, and then when Tooga came by and asked Rooga to go to the movies, he just left!"

"How did that make you feel?" asked my mom.

"Sad, mad, and not very good at all! I wouldn't do that to one of MY friends," I said.

My mom sat down at the kitchen table and told me to sit with her.

"Shooga, sometimes other Oogas forget to follow the Blue Rule and do things that hurt their friends. They don't do this on purpose, but sometimes they need a reminder of the rule," mom said.

"So you think I should tell Rooga how I feel?" I asked.

"I think you will feel better, and Rooga will get the reminder he needs," said my mom.

The next day, I went to Rooga's house to see if he wanted to go to the park. While we walked, I decided to talk to Rooga about the day before.

"Rooga, it really hurt my feelings yesterday that you left the park with Tooga to go to the movies," I said. "Would you like it if he asked me and I left you at the park?"

Rooga was quiet for a minute. Then he said, "You're right, Shooga! I wouldn't want you to treat me that way. I was just so excited to be able to go to the movies, I didn't stop and think how leaving you at the park would make you feel. I'm sorry, Shooga!"

"I forgive you, Rooga. Sometimes we just need a reminder of the Blue Rule. I'm glad I told you how I felt," I said.

We spent the rest of the afternoon at the park,
playing and having fun.

Discussion

1. Do you think it's important to let your friends know when they hurt your feelings? Why or why not?

2. Do you think it's important to admit when you are wrong? Why or why not?

3. Do you think it's important to forgive others when they apologize and admit they were wrong? Why or why not?

4. If someone won't admit they are wrong, what can you do?

About the Author

The story of the Oogas came to Denise at the end of 2009 when she was a teacher for 5th and 6th grade at a middle school in inner city Cleveland. Her students were kicking each other under their table, and she was frustrated that they were not following her number 1 rule in her classroom—Treat others as you want to be treated. She set out to write a children's book that would teach children from a young age how and why to be kind to others. Be sure to check out the Oogas website, www.theoogas.com, where you will find parenting tips, free resources, such as coloring pages, puzzles, and games, and Ooga merchandise! Teachers and homeschool parents, you will find FREE lesson plans and additional discussion questions and activities on the website as well.

Denise has raised four children, most of the time as a single parent. It has been a roller coaster ride to say the least. What has been her saving grace through their teenage years has been her faith. She has learned what unconditional love is and what that looks like in parenting situations.

In her freetime, Denise loves reading realistic fiction, thrillers, Bible studies, and other types of non-fiction books. She also enjoys cooking and baking, especially gluten and dairy free dishes, since she is both gluten and dairy sensitive. You can check out her new website with yummy recipes and health tips at www.dairyfreeandglutenfree.com.

About the Illustrator

Lisa Sutton is a controller at a local company in northeast Ohio. She has earned a Bachelor of Business in Accounting and a Masters of Business Administration. She lives on 50 acres of beautiful land in northeast Ohio with her husband, dog, and cats. Lisa enjoys quilting, cooking, baking, and reading good books.